D0468580

NICHOLI

NICHOLI

BY

COOPER EDENS

ILLUSTRATED BY

A. SCOTT BANFILL

SIMON & SCHUSTER BOOKS FOR YOUNG READERS

Every Christmas Day, our mountain village has a carnival and everyone celebrates the season by building incredible sculptures out of snow.

We've built sculptures of every imaginable kind. But last Christmas the most magical one of all was created . . . though, at first, no one else noticed but me.

The builder was a man known only as Nicholi. He arrived in the late afternoon and went to work right away. It was amazing how fast Nicholi carved his mound of snow.

By the time Nicholi finished his sculpture, a small crowd had gathered around him. With a wave of his hand he invited us to come closer.

He pulled out
the reins and harnesses
he had brought
and asked us to strap,
lace, and buckle them
onto his snow reindeer.

Then Nicholi
lifted each of us,
one by one,
into his
magnificent
snow sleigh.

When Nicholi stepped
into the driver's seat
and picked up the reins,
there was a sudden
swirl of snowflakes.

He then called to his
reindeer, "Yah . . . Hah!"

And before we knew it . . .

. . . we were flying
high above the world,
where the wind whistled
and silver stars sparkled
around a giant moon.

HURRRRRRRRRRRRAY!"
we all cheered
and laughed with joy
as we reached the horizon . . .

. . . and then circled back,
only to be surprised
by another wondrous
sight.

Then, as the mysterious parade
flew off to *who knows where*,
we floated in from the sky
and touched down softly
in an explosion of white.

The ride was over. It was time to go home for Christmas dinner. "Merry Christmas!" we all shouted as Nicholi waved farewell and led his reindeer up the mountain.

But my sister and I
were curious.
So we followed Nicholi
up to the ridge where
the North Wind always
blows,
and there Nicholi's
snow reindeer and sleigh
disappeared.

Then
Nicholi
vanished, too . . .

. . . though my sister
and I believe
that one Christmas
Nicholi is sure to
return.

For Cornelia, Florence, and Minnie Edens
—C. E.
To Grandpa Banfill and the memory of Grandma Banfill
—A. S. B.

SIMON & SCHUSTER BOOKS FOR YOUNG READERS
An imprint of Simon & Schuster Children's Publishing Division
1230 Avenue of the Americas, New York, New York 10020
Text copyright © 1997 by Cooper Edens
Illustrations copyright © 1997 by A. Scott Banfill
All rights reserved including the right of reproduction in whole or in part in any form.
SIMON & SCHUSTER BOOKS FOR YOUNG READERS is a trademark of Simon & Schuster.

Book design by Anahid Hamparian
The text for this book is set in 16-point Italian Garamond
The illustrations are rendered in acrylics
Printed and bound in Hong Kong by South China Printing Company (1988) Ltd.
First Edition
10 9 8 7 6 5 4 3 2 1
Library of Congress Cataloging-in-Publication Data
Edens, Cooper.
Nicholi / by Cooper Edens; illustrated by A. Scott Banfill.
p. cm.
Summary: One Christmas Day in a mountain village, a mysterious man named Nicholi carves a magnificent sleigh and reindeer out of snow and takes the villagers on a magical flight.
ISBN 0-689-80495-4
[1. Christmas—Fiction. 2. Santa Claus—Fiction.] I. Banfill, A. Scott, ill. II. Title.
PZ7.E223Ng 1996
[E]—dc20 94-34340

A NOTE FROM THE ILLUSTRATOR:

I begin by doing thumbnail sketches to work out the general composition of the illustrations. Then I do a rough value study in graphite and a final drawing on vellum. When I'm ready to paint, I first apply a wash of neutral color to an illustration board, either Crescent No. 1 heavyweight or Crescent watercolor board. I use saral transfer paper to transfer the drawing onto the board, and then start painting with Liquitex acrylics that have varying degrees of transparency. I begin with an almost opaque color, then add layer upon layer of transparent colors on top to achieve the desired effect.